FIGHT SCHOOL

JEFF GOTTESFELD

SADDLEBACK
EDUCATIONAL PUBLISHING

red rhino b**oo**ks™

Body Switch	Killer Flood
Clan Castles	The Lost House
The Code	Racer
Flyer	Sky Watchers
Fight School	Standing by Emma
The Garden Troll	Starstruck
Ghost Mountain	Stolen Treasure
The Gift	The Soldier
The Hero of Crow's Crossing	Zombies!
I Am Underdog	Zuze and the Star

With more titles on the way …

SADDLEBACK
EDUCATIONAL PUBLISHING
www.sdlback.com

Copyright ©2015 by Saddleback Educational Publishing
All rights reserved. No part of this book may be reproduced in any form or by any means, electronic or mechanical, including photocopying, recording, scanning, or by any information storage and retrieval system, without the written permission of the publisher. SADDLEBACK EDUCATIONAL PUBLISHING and any associated logos are trademarks and/or registered trademarks of Saddleback Educational Publishing.

ISBN-13: 978-1-62250-919-5
ISBN-10: 1-62250-919-6
eBook: 978-1-63078-045-6

Printed in Guangzhou, China
NOR/1014/CA21401612

19 18 17 16 15   1 2 3 4 5

~~DON~~ DON

Age: 12

Pre-fight Ritual: crushes soda cans

Parents' Jobs: dad is a pro wrestler, and mom is a roller derby team captain

Big Secret: just adopted two rescue kittens

Best Quality: intensity

TOMMY RO~~~~

Age: 12

Favorite School Subject: ~~~rican history

Future Goal: wants to be a sports announcer for ESPN

Favorite Food: breakfast burritos

Best Quality: eager to learn

1
THE BIG NEWS

Mr. Fay used to be a mixed martial arts pro. Now he ran Stars MMA Fight School for kids. MMA was mixed martial arts. Mr. Fay's voice was as big as his body. And he had a giant beard.

"Be strong!" he yelled at the kids. "Strong body. Strong mind. Strong heart. This is not a place for wimps. This is a fight school! Whose fight school?"

Tommy Robbins stood there. He was twelve. He had been coming to Stars MMA for two years. Tommy loved Mr. Fay. All the kids did. He was a great teacher. But Mr. Fay had never acted like this before.

"I said, 'Whose school?' No answer?" Mr. Fay pumped a fist. "Twenty push-ups!"

Tommy looked at Ben Wong. Ben was his

good bud. They were the best in the class.

Tommy had the best skills. Tommy was the best puncher. He was the best kicker. He was the fastest. But he was not as good in a fight as Ben. Ben could beat guys twice his size. Tommy was always good in drills. But he lost when it mattered. It was like he had a mental block. He could not focus. He choked.

Some kids said MMA was bad news. But Tommy knew better. MMA was hard. It hurt to get kicked. Or hit. The goal of fight school was to make a strong body. A strong mind. A strong heart. The kids all wore pads. And there was always a ref on the mat.

MY TRAINING GEAR

← KNEE PADS

HEADGEAR

GLOVES →

← MOUTH GUARD

"Push-ups!" Ben called to the other kids. He and Tommy were the fight school leaders. "Do them!"

Tommy and Ben dropped to the mat. The other kids did too. Tommy did twenty fast push-ups. So did Ben. They were done before anyone else.

"Good, Ben and Tommy," Mr. Fay told them. "The rest of you? Come on! Move it! Faster."

The others did their reps. Tommy was friends with three of them. Mac, Shelly, and Hugo. They were great kids. Hugo was good at math. Shelly was an artist. Mac could sing. They were at fight school to get strong.

Mr. Fay's voice got nicer. "Good job. Did I scare you? Put you off your game? Make it hard to focus? Focus is the key to MMA. And to life. When I ask whose fight school? There is only one answer. *'Our fight school.'* Whose fight school?"

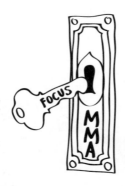

The kids shouted, "Our fight school!"

"That's right," Mr. Fay nodded. "Here, we focus."

Tommy bit his lip. Mr. Fay always said Tommy had the skill to beat anyone. But focus was hard for Tommy. His mind would go here and there. He would always choke.

"Sit down." All the kids sat in a circle. "I have news. About Saturday night. It's good. Great, even."

Saturday night was a big MMA show in the city. Mr. Fay was taking all the kids. The arena would be packed.

THIS SATURDAY

MMA SHOW

@ THE BIG ARENA

Mr. Fay kept talking. "Here's the news about the MMA show. One of you will fight too. I just have to choose who it will be."

Tommy hoped it would be him. But he was also scared. What if he choked?

2
CRUSHED!

Mr. Fay explained. The MMA show would have one kids' fight. The kids would be sixth graders. One fighter would come from Stars. The other would be from Bad Dudes MMA. It was across town.

DON
- MAKES 4th GRADERS CRY
- GREW 2 FEET IN 3 MONTHS

The BAD DUDES

AGE
- EATS RAW EGGS FOR BREAKFAST
- KICKS EVERY TRASH CAN OVER

CALVIN
- SPITS MUD
- FLUSHED 13 GOLDFISH DOWN THE TOLIET

Tommy was excited. To be in the show would be cool. But if he were Mr. Fay, he would pick Ben.

"Let's see who will be our rep." Mr. Fay looked at Ben. Tommy thought that was it. Then Mr. Fay looked at Tommy. "Ben? Tommy? Suit up! Let's settle it on the mat."

Tommy got to his feet. This was a great chance. He could take Ben. He had to stay calm. Think of one thing at a time. Not choke.

Tommy put on his headgear, pads, and gloves. MMA fighting was wide open. He could kick. He could punch. He could use an elbow. Or a knee. He could wrestle. And so could Ben.

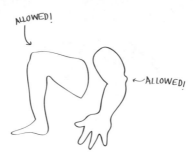

ALLOWED!

←ALLOWED!

The pads stopped kids from getting hurt. The best way to win in MMA was by "tap out." A tap out was when one person tapped the mat or the other person. A tap out said, "I quit." There were holds that caused tap outs. Tommy's best one was the arm lock. He'd had it done to him. It felt like his arm was ready to break.

There would be a big crowd at the arena. Huge. His mom and dad would come. His big brother, Rich. Tons of kids. He could be cheered. But what if he lost? He could be booed.

Tommy tried to focus on Ben. But his mind was racing. So many hopes. Dreams. But most of all, fears.

Mr. Fay blew a whistle. Tommy turned. The kids had formed a ring. Ben was in his gear. Tommy looked at him. Ben was a bit bigger than Tommy.

There were two types of MMA fighters. There were strikers. They were good at punching and kicking. Tommy was a striker.

There were grapplers. They were good if the fight went to the mat. Ben was a grappler.

Tommy had to keep Ben from taking him down. He would try a punch-kick combo.

COMBO!

That might bring Ben down. Then he could lock Ben into a tap out.

"I can do this," Tommy told himself. "I can do this."

But his mind still raced. He saw himself in the MMA cage—

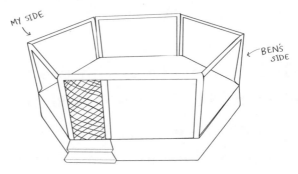

MY SIDE

BEN'S SIDE

"Ready?" Mr. Fay asked.

"Ready!" Ben called

"Ready!" Tommy agreed. He felt anything but ready. He had to calm down. Now. Focus—

"Fight!"

Ben came at Tommy. A spinning hook

kick. Two quick punches to Tommy's face. Then a jumping front kick. It hit Tommy in the face.

Tommy came back with two left hooks and a jab. Those moves missed. He tried to think what to do.

"Come on, Tommy. Figure him out!" Mr. Fay called. Other kids shouted too. Tommy tried to listen. The more he listened, the worse he did.

"Focus," he told himself. Why was he so good in drills? Why was he so bad in a fight?

Ben came at him again. He grabbed Tommy. Tommy tried to get away. He failed.

Ben put a leg behind him. Then pushed. It was a perfect trip. Tommy fell. Then Ben got Tommy's left arm in a lock.

Ow! It hurt so much.

Tommy tapped out. The fight was over.

The kids were dead quiet. Tommy knew why.

It was one thing to lose. It was another to get crushed.

Tommy had just been crushed.

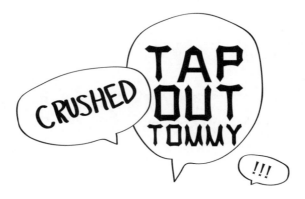

3
VISITOR

Tommy showered when he got home. Then he came downstairs. His brother, Rich, was making dinner. Rich was five years older. "What's up, little brother? How come so sad?"

SOMETIMES RICH MAKES THE BEST BREAKFAST FOR DINNER

Tommy tried to smile. "I look sad?"

"Like a girl broke your heart. But you're twelve. So that's out. What's going on?"

Tommy grinned. He had the best brother. Some big brothers were mean. Rich only ever wanted the best for him.

"Well. I lost today at fight school."

"So?" Rich led them to the kitchen. There was pizza in the oven. It smelled good.

HURRY UP AND BE DONE!

"I lost to Ben."

Rich opened the oven to check the pizza.

"Four more minutes. You lost to Ben. So what? You always lose to Ben."

"I know. I'm sick of it. It was a big match. To be in the MMA show on Saturday."

Rich washed his hands at the sink. "That's gotta hurt."

Tommy put some plates on the table. "So, Ben's in. I'm out."

"Hey. At least he's your bud."

"Yeah, I'm happy for him. But still …"

"I know," Rich said. He dried his hands. "You wanted it. How come you lost?"

Tommy made two fists. "I'm good with these." Then he tapped his own head. "But I'm bad with this."

IS THIS THING ON?

"So. You choked," Rich said.

Tommy nodded. He did not like to admit it. "Something like that."

"You're scared," Rich suggested.

Tommy shook his head. He was not scared. He had good skills. It was something else. "Nope. No fear. But no focus."

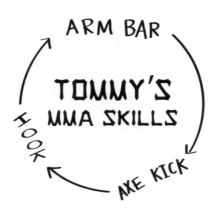

"Don't feel bad. You'll have other chances." Rich put the towel back on the rack.

"You don't get it, Rich. Not like—"

The doorbell rang.

Rich made a face. "Can you see who that is, Tommy?"

The doorbell rang again. Tommy ran and opened it. To his surprise, it was Mr. Fay. He wore jeans and a nice shirt. He smiled and touched his beard. "Ah. I'm in the right place. Hi, Tommy."

MR. FAY'S BEARD IS SO **BIG**

I THINK THIS LIVES IN IT

"Hi, Mister Fay."

"Your parents here?"

Tommy shook his head. "Just my brother. We're about to eat."

Mr. Fay frowned. "I was hoping to

see your folks. There is a problem. With Saturday night. For the MMA show. When will your mom and dad be here?"

Tommy looked up the street. His dad's car was coming. Mom was in it too. "You're in luck. That's my mom and dad. They're coming now."

"Great! They'll want to hear what I have to say. I know they will." Mr. Fay stared at him. "You, Tommy? You? I'm not so sure."

4
FEAR THE BATHROOM

It was an odd group at the kitchen table. Tommy. Rich. Their parents. Mr. Fay.

Mr. Fay had been at their house two years ago. When Tommy learned about fight school, he begged to go. But his parents said no way. Rich had stuck up for Tommy.

He even asked Mr. Fay to come meet their parents. Then they agreed. But just for a tryout. That tryout changed Tommy's life.

"Thank you for having me," Mr. Fay said.

"Always glad to see you, Mister Fay. What brings you out?" Tommy's dad asked.

"Tommy had a bad day on the mat. Isn't that right, Tommy?"

Tommy felt his face burn. He nodded. "Yeah."

"Excuse me, Tommy?"

Tommy winced. Mr. Fay hated the word "yeah." Tommy knew it.

"Yes. I did."

Mr. Fay turned to Tommy's parents. "He fought with Ben to see who would be in the MMA show. Ben beat him. It's a problem."

Tommy's father rubbed his chin. "Ben always beats Tommy. So what's the problem?"

Ugh. Tommy felt bad to hear his dad say that. But it was true. Ben *did* always beat him.

Mr. Fay looked right at Tommy. "The problem is this. When Ben got home, he slipped. The bathroom floor was wet. He broke his right leg."

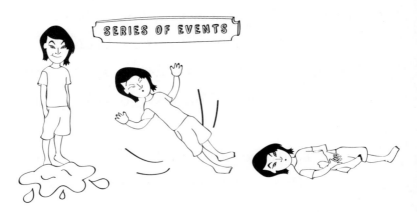

SERIES OF EVENTS

"What?" Tommy yelped. "Is this a joke?"

"It's no joke," Mr. Fay said. "Fear the bathroom. He's at the ER now. His mom called. He can't fight."

"So who will …"

Tommy stopped talking. He understood the problem. Stars MMA needed a sub. The next best person was Tommy. No one else was even half as good. It would not be fair to put Hugo, Shelly, or Mac in the ring. They were good kids. So were the others in the class. Everyone loved MMA. But Tommy had the skills.

There was only one kid who could do it.

But the crowd. The noise. How could he keep his head on straight?

MMA Fans are wild!

"Tommy?" Mr. Fay asked. "Can you do this?"

Tommy looked to his big brother. Rich smiled at him.

"Tommy, I know how hard big fights are for you. But this is your chance to change that," Rich said. "Take it."

Tommy looked at Mr. Fay. Rich was right.

"Okay," he told Mr. Fay. "I'm in."

5
THE KILLER

Before Tommy went to bed, he texted Ben.

"Bad break, dude."

"Funny," Ben replied

"How long until u are back?"

"6 to 8 weeks. Too bad I can't kick with this!"

"U know I'm doing MMA on Sat."

"Will b there. Good luck. Can I ask u something?"

"Yep."

It took a moment for Ben's text to come.

THINGS I COULD'VE DONE WHILE WAITING FOR BEN'S TEXT

games   haircut   clean behind the couch

"Why were u so lame today?"

Tommy lied, "U were 2 good."

"Nope. U beat u. U always beat u."

That was true. He felt bad about it. But he now had a second chance. If he could just make the most of it.

The next day at school was hard. The word was out. He was in the MMA event. That was cool. But everyone heard why. That was not cool.

EVEN OUR JANITOR HEARD

SAM

Tommy saw Ben at lunch. He had a cast on his left leg. All the kids signed it. Tommy was last. He tried to be funny.

Finally found a way to stop you! Tommy.

Ben grinned. "You're going to need to stop more than me."

"I've got a week to prep," Tommy told him.

"You know who you're in the cage with?"

Tommy shook his head. "No clue."

"I saw who it is. It's on the Bad Dudes website. Some guy named Don Moore. I hate to say it. He looks mean. He looks strong. Tommy? He looks like a killer."

6
LOSER!

After math class, Tommy went to the library. He went to the computer station. Ben was right. Right there on the Bad Dudes website. Don Moore. He was big. He was ugly. He had a shaved head. He even had a tattoo.

Tommy wondered what mom or dad would let a sixth grader do that. Not many. His heart sank. He wondered if he could last twenty seconds with this guy.

That afternoon at fight school, Mr. Fay took him aside. "You saw this Don guy?"

"Yes, sir."

"You need a plan."

"Yes, sir."

"What's your plan?" Mr. Fay asked.

"I don't have a clue."

"Then sit down. Think of one."

Tommy looked up at him. "Can you help me? Please."

To his surprise, Mr. Fay shook his head. "No. I want you to do this on your own."

Tommy started to get angry. "But you're my coach!"

THINGS A COACH SHOULD DO:

1. MOTIVATE
2. TEACH
3. HELP KIDS!
CLEAN MATS *BONUS

Mr. Fay shook his head. "Your coach is telling you to think of a fight plan. MMA is not just about a strong body. It's about your mind. And your heart. Get to it."

Mr. Fay went into the office. When he

came back to the mat, he was with a teen guy. This kid was as big as Don. Maybe even bigger. "Tommy, meet Lou Dalton. He's in high school. He's going to get you ready. Take Lou down. Then you can take Don."

The kids near Tommy laughed. Tommy did not think it was funny. Mac and Hugo came over to talk.

"You're fighting Lou?" Hugo asked. "He can school you!"

Mac nodded. "No offense, Tommy. I wish

36

Ben was our guy. You always choke."

Someone shouted from near the door. "Shut your face, Mac!"

Tommy turned. It was Ben. He was on crutches. He couldn't train. But he had come to fight school anyway. That was so like him. It was great to see him. But there was no time to chat. He had to spar with Lou.

ALMOST DIDN'T SEE HIM!

The kids formed a ring. Tommy had a plan. He would try to keep Lou away with kicks. He would aim for Lou's body. He would move in and out. Lou was bigger. But maybe Tommy could be faster. He would try a two-leg takedown. Then maybe an ankle lock to get Lou to tap out.

It was a good plan. But Mr. Fay made it hard for Tommy. He told the kids to root for Lou. In fact, they even yelled at Tommy.

"Yo! Tommy! You suck! Tommy! You're lame!"

"Tommy! You're gonna lose!"

Ben cheered. But it did not help. Tommy lost focus. His plan to beat Lou fell apart.

He punched wildly. Then Lou came in low for a takedown. Tommy fell to the mat. Lou put Tommy in a leg slicer. Tommy's right leg felt like it was going to fall off.

Tommy tapped out.

Again, he was the loser. Again, he had barely put up a fight.

"Loser!" someone yelled.

7
IN THE CAGE

Tommy worked all week. He worked with Lou. He worked with Mr. Fay. But he always lost focus. The worst was when kids yelled advice to him. He tried not to listen. But he could not shut out the voices. He did not know whether to kick, punch, defend, or attack. He went from bad to worse.

Ben tried to pump him up. "You can do this."

"I am trying."

On Friday, Tommy and Ben went to fight school. The next night was the MMA show. But there would be no more practicing.

"No mat work today. Tommy needs to rest. We're going on a field trip. Come on."

Everyone got in a van. Mr. Fay drove into the city. Tommy was amazed where they ended up. They were at the big arena. It was where Tommy would fight.

The kids followed Mr. Fay to the floor. Tommy hung back with Ben. His bud was still slow on his crutches.

"Can I tell you the truth?" Ben asked.

"Sure."

"I'm worried." Ben scanned the arena. "This place is gonna be full of people. They'll all be going crazy. How are you gonna focus?"

Tommy shook his head. "Dude? That's not helpful."

"It's the truth. You need an edge."

"Maybe Don will break his leg."

Ben grinned. "I doubt it. He has legs of steel."

LEGS
OF
STEEL

Boxing matches took place in a ring. Pro MMA matches took place in a cage. The cage was up for the show. It had six sides. Mr. Fay took the kids inside the cage. Tommy looked out at the seats. They would be full of fans. Stomping feet. Clapping hands. Yelling stuff. He got dizzy at the idea of fighting.

HEY!
CAN I EAT DINNER IN PEACE?

"Hi, guys."

A small, powerful man stepped into the cage. He wore black pants and a green shirt. Tommy knew who he was. Everyone did. This was Nate Nitehawk. He had been an MMA champ. He didn't fight anymore because he had a bad knee.

This was so cool. They were going to meet the great Nate Nitehawk.

"Hiya, Nate." Mr. Fay greeted him like a friend. The kids stared. Nate was an MMA legend.

"Hey, George." Nate called Mr. Fay by his first name. Whoa.

"Thanks for coming to help me out. Want to meet my kids?"

The kids lined up. Nate went down the line. He asked each kid their name. Then he shook hands. Tommy was last. He was so excited to meet Nate. He barely got his name out.

MR. FAY'S WALLET

Nate grinned when he was done. "So, George? Which of your guys will be in this cage?"

"Tommy," Mr. Fay called. "The last guy you met."

Nate stepped over to Tommy. "You're Tommy, right?"

"Yeah," Tommy said.

"Yes. Not yeah. Yes," Mr. Fay corrected.

"Yes. Sir."

Nate turned to the other kids. "Guys? Clear out. George? You too. I want two people in this cage. Me and Tommy. That okay with you, Tommy? We have a few things to talk about."

This was nuts. Here he was, face-to-face with Nate Nitehawk. Nate wanted him alone in the cage for a talk. Was it okay with him? It was more than okay. It was great.

8
THE CHAMP

"How does it feel to be in here?" Nate asked.

"Scary. Like I don't belong," Tommy said. The arena seemed huge. He felt so small.

ALSO SCARY LIKE...

Spiders

clowns

Rich's dirty gym socks

"Yeah. I know that feeling. Mister Fay says you have skills."

Tommy shrugged. "But I choke."

"We'll see about that. Let's do some work. Out of those shoes."

They each took off their shoes. Tommy faced the champ.

"Take me down," Nate told Tommy.

"You're kidding."

Nate shook his head. "Nope. Take me down. What's the best way?"

Tommy thought a second. With a big guy like Nate, the best way was to get behind him. Drive his knees forward. Then Tommy could trip him. Nate would face-plant.

FACE-PLANT?

"I could—"

"Don't say it," Nate told him. "Do it."

Tommy did it.

To his shock, Nate went down face-first. A second later, he was up on his feet.

WHOOOSH

"Faster," Nate advised. "Do it again."

Tommy did it again. Faster. Nate went down one more time.

"Again. Much faster. And try some other moves too."

For the next ten minutes, Tommy took

Nate down. He did it twenty ways. He focused. The only thing in the world was him, Nate, and the mat.

"Good," Nate told him. "Now, one more time. End it with an arm bar."

Tommy did. The champ's cry of pain was real. He tapped out. Then he grinned. That's what you'll do against Don."

Tommy shook his head sadly. "Are you kidding? He'll fight back. There'll be all these people screaming."

Nate grinned. "The crowd gets to you? The yelling?"

Tommy nodded. "Yup. It's like I have super ears."

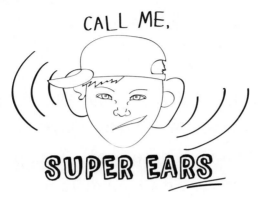

CALL ME,

SUPER EARS

"It happened to me. Back when I was starting out. I know what to do about that. Try these."

Tommy watched as Nate dug into his pants pocket. Then he opened his hand to show Tommy what he had.

Earplugs. Two foam earplugs.

Tommy cracked up. "I should wear those in the cage?"

Nate shrugged. "Why not?"

HAVE THESE BEEN USED?

"Hey, hey!" Mr. Fay led the class back onto the arena floor. "Who won?"

"No winner," Nate said. "Just practice." He put out his fist to bump Tommy. Tommy fist-bumped with him.

"See you tomorrow," Nate told him.

"Thanks, champ."

On the ride back to fight school, Tommy sat next to Ben. He didn't say much. The work with Nate had helped. But he was still worried. Don Moore was so big. He closed his eyes. It did not help. There was a movie in his mind. It was him and Don in the cage. Don had him down. Don was punching him. The ref watched. Tommy tapped out. But the punches kept coming.

"Hey! Check this out."

Tommy opened his eyes. "What?"

Ben was looking at him. "What were you just thinking about?"

Tommy sighed. "Getting my butt kicked."

Ben poked him with his elbow. "Well, I think I can stop that. Look." Ben tapped his phone a few times. Up came a video. He gave his phone to Tommy.

Tommy started the video. It was a fight

film of Don Moore. Tommy watched him crush a smaller kid with just five kicks and four punches.

"How'd you find this?" Tommy asked.

"Google. He probably doesn't even know it's there."

Tommy moaned. "Great. What a big help. The guy is a killer. He's gonna kill me."

Ben shook a finger at him. "Don't you get it? He's a striker. Just like you. We can study this. We can figure out how to beat the guy."

9
FIGHT NIGHT

Fight night!

The arena was packed. The fights were great. The fight school kids and parents were in a special area. That was when Tommy saw Don for the first time. He seemed bigger than in the video. He wore all black. Tommy wore a red shirt and jeans.

"He's huge," Tommy told Ben.

"That's good. The crowd roots for the smaller guy. The bigger they come? The harder they fall, right?" Ben took a selfie with Tommy, then checked it out. "Look at yourself! You're as tight as a zip line. You need to relax. We have a plan. Remember?"

"Okay. I'll try." Tommy set his jaw. He took big breaths. In. Out. In. Out. He had worked hard. He had been in the cage with Nate Nitehawk. He had studied the video. He saw that Don punched well and kicked better. But he had bad footwork. Tommy needed to be fast. Speed was the key to winning.

DON HAS **BAD** FOOTWORK

A half-hour before the main event, he said good-bye to his buds. Then he went to a dressing room with Mr. Fay. Nate was there. So was Rich. It was quiet. Mr. Fay and Nate got him ready. Tommy put on shorts and a white shirt. Both had the Stars MMA logo. He fastened his headgear.

"You good to go?" Mr. Fay asked.

"I'm good," Tommy said.

"Don't forget the ears," Nate told him.

"Oops! You're right."

"Forget what?" Mr. Fay asked.

Tommy found his earplugs. He took off the headgear, put them in, and put the headgear back in place. "That. So I don't hear the crowd."

Mr. Fay blinked. "I should have thought of that."

Nate laughed. "That's why I was a champ, George. And you never were."

Tommy took a moment with his brother.

"Stick to the plan," Rich said.

Tommy nodded. He was ready. This time, he would not choke.

The call came in on the P.A. "Tommy Robbins? Tommy Robbins to the cage!"

Don was in the cage when Tommy stepped into the arena. "From the Stars MMA Fight School, meet Tommy Robbins!"

There were a lot of cheers. Ben was right. The crowd rooted for Tommy. He smiled a grim smile as the ref talked rules and safety. There would be two rounds of one minute each.

The crowd went nuts as the ref moved Tommy and Don to the center.

They touched gloves. The fight was on.

10
TAP OUT

Don came at Tommy like a human tank.
He wrapped Tommy in his huge arms.

Tommy panicked. This was all wrong. He
had seen the video. Don was a striker. He
was no grappler. Yet here he was, stuck in

Don's grip. He had made the wrong plan. He was set for the wrong kind of fighter.

The crowd went crazy. Don pushed him to the cage wall. Tommy tried to slip out of his arms. Then Don went for a choke hold. This was bad. Don's right arm was around Tommy's neck. Tommy only had a few seconds before he would go weak. He pushed back with his head. Then he pushed on Don's left elbow.

Tommy was free. But he had no time to be happy. Don came at him. Tommy threw some jabs. Don blocked them. He kicked with his left foot. Don danced away. Then Don came in with bull rush. He wanted a takedown.

Don got around him again. He put Tommy on his hip. He set up a hip throw. It was a classic judo move. Tommy crashed to the mat. The crowd moaned.

Don was on him. He wanted an arm lock. He had it. The fans roared. They wanted Tommy to stay strong. He tried not to tap out, but it hurt so much—

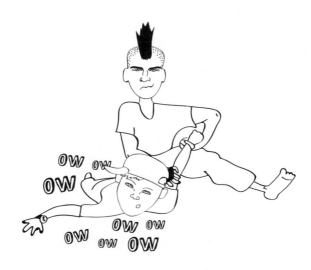

The bell sounded. The round was over. Tommy was saved.

Tommy went to his chair. Mr. Fay was there. "That was almost it."

"Yeah," Tommy agreed. "I mean, yes."

"Tommy? In the middle of an MMA bout? 'Yeah' is okay. How do you feel?"

"I feel good. But I need a new plan. He's a grappler."

"Focus, then."

Tommy closed his eyes. He saw himself in the ring. Not with Don. But with Ben. He had always tried to beat Ben with his fists and feet. But what if …

He had it! His plan. It was worth a try.

The arena buzzed for the last round.

The ref called them to the center. The boys touched gloves. The crowd went crazy. The round began.

Tommy came at Don like ten tanks.

It was kind of nuts. He was no grappler. Tommy lived on speed, not power. But Don was so shocked that he froze. Tommy spun behind him, just like he had with Nate. Don tried to turn to his right, to face Tommy. Tommy had hoped for this. He moved his right leg against Don's right ankle. Then he pushed.

Down went Don.

The crowd roared. Tommy heard it through his earplugs. Don put up his left arm to ward Tommy off. Tommy grabbed it. He put his knees across Don's chest. Don tried to fight him. Tommy held on. He got Don's left arm between his legs. Then he pushed down on the arm against his hip. Arm bar!

Don screamed in pain. Then he tapped out.

Tommy was stunned. He had won!

He got to his feet. The ref raised his arm. The crowd cheered. Tommy just stood there. He had looked defeat in the face. He had not choked. Best of all, Mr. Fay had let him figure it out by himself.

Don came over and hugged him. "That

took guts, man."

"You almost beat me."

"Rematch sometime?"

"You got it," Tommy said. "You earned it, dude."

Then everyone he loved was in the ring with him. Mr. Fay. Nate Nitehawk. Ben. His friends. His family. He had done it. He had learned so much this week. About his own strong body. His mind. And most of all, about his heart.

That was why they called it fight school. It was not just a school for MMA. It was a school for life.